"Why can't I stay here?" he asked.

"I'm sorry, Eddie, but I have to work," Mama explained. "But you will like staying with Auntie. She will make you delicious matooke."

"I don't like matooke," Eddie said crossly.

Mama smiled. "You'll love Auntie's matooke."

To get to Auntie's house, they had to go on a big bus that went very slowly.

Then they had to ride on a boda-boda along a track that was very bumpy.

"Look at all the monkeys!" Eddie shouted.

Matooke

by Tracy Turner-Jones and reminac kc

W

FRANKLIN WATTS

LONDON • SYDNEY

Eddie lived with his mama in a block of flats in the city. It was the school holidays and Eddie was going to stay with his auntie and cousin Susan in the countryside for the first time.

Eddie did not want to go to the countryside. He wanted to stay in the city and go skateboarding with his friends.

Auntie and cousin Susan were waiting outside
their house. They hugged Mama and Eddie.
Eddie was sad when it was time for
Mama to go.
"I will be back soon," she promised.
Eddie, Auntie and Susan waved until
they couldn't see Mama anymore.

5

Auntie made Eddie and Susan a warm cup of spicy chai. They sat on the porch to drink it.

"Now," said Auntie, "it's time to sweep up the leaves in the yard."

But Eddie really wanted to swing on the hammock.

"Come on," said Susan. "We have to sweep the leaves so we can put them in the basket."

So Eddie swept leaves with Auntie and Susan.

Soon there was a big pile of leaves.

"Now we have to put the leaves in the basket so we can take them to the plantation," Auntie said.

Eddie didn't want to pick up the leaves. He was worried he would get his new T-shirt dirty.

"Why do we have to go to the plantation?" Eddie asked.

"You'll see," said Auntie, with a grin.

Eddie grabbed some leaves and threw them into the basket.

Finally, the basket was full.

"You two carry the basket," Auntie said,

"and I will bring my rake in the wheelbarrow."

"When we get to the plantation, we can put

the leaves into the ground," Susan said.

"Didn't we just take the leaves **off** the ground?"

Eddie asked. But he wanted to help Auntie, so

he lifted the basket with Susan and off they

went.

9

On the plantation, there were lots of very tall matooke plants. As they walked between the plants, Eddie heard a rustling noise.

"Was that a snake?" he said.

"Are you scared of snakes?" Susan asked.

"No, of course not," Eddie said.

"Don't be afraid, Eddie. There aren't any snakes," Auntie said, laughing. "It's just a bird."

The ground in the plantation was all soft and spongy. Eddie wished he hadn't worn his favourite trainers.

At the end of the row of plants, Auntie's friend Frank was cutting down matooke. Frank told the children to tip the leaves onto the ground around the matooke plants.

"The leaves are good for the matooke," he said.

Auntie used her rake to push the leaves into the soil.

"We push the leaves into the ground to feed the trees," she told Eddie.

"Jump on the leaves with me, Eddie!" said Susan, laughing. "Then Frank can give us some matooke!"

Eddie didn't feel like jumping, so he stamped on the leaves very hard instead.

He stamped faster and faster. Susan jumped and Eddie stamped. He liked stamping. It was fun!

"Thank you for bringing the leaves for the trees," Frank said. "Now you can choose a bunch of matooke to take home for your dinner." Auntie took some matooke and put it in the wheelbarrow. Eddie helped push the wheelbarrow back to Auntie's house.

"And now," said Auntie, "It is time to cook the matooke."
Eddie followed Auntie and Susan into their kitchen.
"Erm ... Auntie?" he said. "I don't really like matooke."
"You'll love my matooke," Auntie said, grinning.

She made a fire under a big pot.

Then she peeled the matooke and ground up the spices. The children chopped the vegetables and put them into the pot. Eddie liked stirring as the vegetables sizzled.

"Thank you," said Auntie. "Now you can go and play while the matooke cooks."

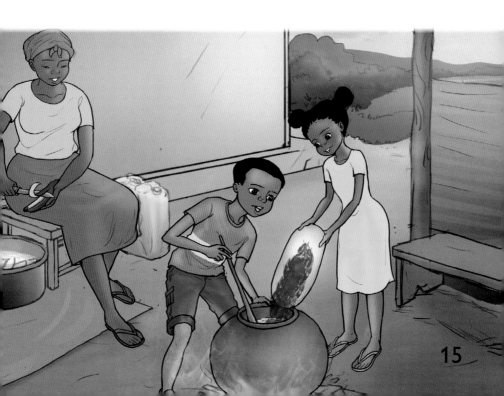

A little bit later, Eddie smelled something

very sweet and spicy.

"Dinner time," Auntie called.

"Eddie told me he doesn't want any,"

Susan said.

But the wonderful smell made

Eddie's mouth water.

"Well, I **am** hungry," he said. "I will try

a little bite."

Eddie tried a bit of the food on his plate.

Then he tried a bit more. Then he ate it all up.

"**That** was matooke?" he asked.

"Yes!" Auntie and Susan said together.

17

Suddenly Eddie pushed back his chair and ran to get a broom.

"What are you doing?" asked Auntie.

Eddie smiled. "I'm going to sweep up more leaves," he said.

"Why?" asked Susan.

"So I can take the leaves to the plantation and give them to the trees," Eddie replied. "Then when Mama comes, we can have some more matooke."

"But you don't like matooke," said Auntie and Susan, laughing.

"Yes, I do!" said Eddie, smiling.

"I **love** matooke!"

Story order

Look at these 5 pictures and captions.
Put the pictures in the right order
to retell the story.

1

Eddie stamps on the leaves.

2

They prepare matooke together.